Dear Parent:

Congratulations! Your child is taking the first steps on an exciting journey. The destination? Independent reading!

STEP INTO READING® will help your child get there. The program offers books at five levels that accompany children from their first attempts at reading to reading success. Each step includes fun stories, fiction and nonfiction, and colorful art. There are also Step into Reading Sticker Books, Step into Reading Math Readers, and Step into Reading Phonics Readers—a complete literacy program with something to interest every child.

Learning to Read, Step by Step!

Ready to Read   Preschool–Kindergarten
• big type and easy words • rhyme and rhythm • picture clues
For children who know the alphabet and are eager to begin reading.

Reading with Help   Preschool–Grade 1
• basic vocabulary • short sentences • simple stories
For children who recognize familiar words and sound out new words with help.

Reading on Your Own   Grades 1–3
• engaging characters • easy-to-follow plots • popular topics
For children who are ready to read on their own.

Reading Paragraphs   Grades 2–3
• challenging vocabulary • short paragraphs • exciting stories
For newly independent readers who read simple sentences with confidence.

Ready for Chapters   Grades 2–4
• chapters • longer paragraphs • full-color art
For children who want to take the plunge into chapter books but still like colorful pictures.

STEP INTO READING® is designed to give every child a successful reading experience. The grade levels are only guides. Children can progress through the steps at their own speed, developing confidence in their reading, no matter what their grade.

Remember, a lifetime love of reading starts with a single step!

To Marion and Lavern Boelts, with love
—M.B.

For Richard and Nicole
—J.G.

Text copyright © 2003 by Maribeth Boelts. Illustrations copyright © 2003 by Jan Gerardi.
All rights reserved under International and Pan-American Copyright Conventions. Published
in the United States by Random House Children's Books, a division of Random House, Inc.,
New York, and simultaneously in Canada by Random House of Canada Limited, Toronto.

www.stepintoreading.com

Educators and librarians, for a variety of teaching tools, visit us at
www.randomhouse.com/teachers

Library of Congress Cataloging-in-Publication Data
Boelts, Maribeth.
The Sloths get a pet / by Maribeth Boelts ; illustrated by Jan Gerardi.
   p.   cm. — (Step into reading. A step 3 book)
SUMMARY: The Sloth family falls in love with the sleepy puppy at the pet store, but when they
bring him home, they are surprised to find out he's a bundle of energy and not at all what
they bargained for.
ISBN 0-375-81229-6 (trade) — ISBN 0-375-91229-0 (lib. bdg.)
[1. Sloths—Fiction.   2. Dogs—Fiction.   3. Animals—Infancy—Fiction.   4. Pets—Fiction.]
I. Gerardi, Jan, ill.   II. Title.   III. Series: Step into reading. Step 3 book.
PZ7.B6338 Sl 2003   [E]—dc21   2003000988

Printed in the United States of America First Edition 10 9 8 7 6 5 4 3 2

STEP INTO READING, RANDOM HOUSE, and the Random House colophon are registered trademarks
of Random House, Inc.

The Sloths Get a Pet

by Maribeth Boelts

illustrated by Jan Gerardi

Random House 🏠 New York

Once there was

a family of sloths.

Papa Sloth worked
as a bed tester.

Mama Sloth worked
as a model
in a pajamas store.

Stanley and Stella Sloth

were in the second grade.

They liked

quiet reading time,

rest time,

and science film time.

One day, Stella came home
with a library book.
It was all about pets.
"Let's get a pet," Stella said.

Mama and Papa
yawned and stretched.
"Yes, let's get a pet,"
they said.

On Saturday,

the Sloths woke up early.

The pet store was one block away.

The Sloths took the bus.

But they slept through their stop!

They woke up many hours later.

"Ah, here's our stop," said Papa.

The pet store was almost

ready to close.

The Sloth family shuffled past the turtles.

"Too slow," Papa said.

They crawled past the fish tanks.

"Too boring," Mama said.

Then Stella called

from over in the corner,

"Here is the perfect pet!"

In the cage

was a sleeping puppy.

The pet store owner

began turning off the lights.

"We'll take him," Mama said.

The next day was Sunday.

The Sloths rested.

The puppy rested, too.

"He is perfect," Stella said.

"He is the best," Stanley said.

"What shall we name him?"

asked Mama.

Papa sighed.

"Too much thinking.

He can be Puppy for now."

The puppy-care chores

seemed simple.

Papa cut a hole in the door.

Now Puppy could go

out and in

anytime he wanted.

Mama ordered 300 pounds
of puppy food.

Stanley filled up
the wading pool.
Puppy had plenty of
water to drink.

Stella tied strings

to all of Puppy's toys.

She could throw them

and pull them back.

As Puppy grew,
he started to do
many new things.
One of those things
was called chewing.

"My blanket!" Stella cried.

"My pillow!" Mama cried.

"My eyeshade!" Papa cried.

"My sleepy-songs tape!"
Stanley cried.

"BAD DOG!" cried the Sloths.

Puppy also did something
called running around.
Puppy ran around the sofa,
behind the chair,

down the hall,

under the table,

and in and out of
the puppy door
all day and night.

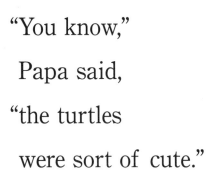

"You know,"
Papa said,
"the turtles
were sort of cute."

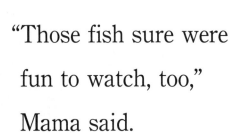

"Those fish sure were
fun to watch, too,"
Mama said.

Each day, the Sloth family

went to work and school.

Then they came home

to Puppy and his messes.

One day, they came home

and there was just a mess.

But no Puppy.

They called for him.

"Puppy!"

"Oh, Mess-Maker!"

"Oh, Ankle-Biter!"

"Oh, Piddle-Puddler!"

They laughed.

Then they listened.

Then they looked.

Puppy was gone!

Outside, the rain began.

Thunder boomed.

Lightning flashed.

The Sloth family put on
their raincoats and boots.
They grabbed their flashlight.
They went out into the storm
to find Puppy.

They sloshed through the alley.

They splashed through the street.

They slimed through the mud.

Puppy was nowhere to be found.

The tired and hungry Sloths

went back home.

The next day, the Sloths went
to school and work, as usual.

They all had a terrible day.
Papa tossed and turned
on the beds.

Mama could not stand still.

Stanley and Stella

could not rest

at rest time.

That night, the Sloths
climbed into
their giant hammock.

"Puppy was the
cutest puppy ever,"
Stella said.
"He didn't chew *everything*,"
Stanley said.

Papa began to sniffle.

Mama heard
Papa's sniffle.
She began to whimper.

Stella and Stanley

began to cry.

The whole Sloth family

was sobbing.

"Oh, Puppy! Where are you?"

Then they heard a sound.

Was it tiny toenails clicking

on the porch?

A tiny brown-and-white face

peeked through

the hole in the door.

"PUPPY!" they shouted.

"YOU CAME BACK!"

Puppy danced, jumped,

and wagged his tail.

In his mouth, he had a page

from Stella's pet book.

Papa read the page out loud.

"CARING FOR YOUR PUPPY.

Walk your puppy every day.

Play with your puppy

so he does not become lonely.

Treat your puppy as a

member of the family."

Stanley shook his head.

"We did not do those things."

The Sloths felt bad.

They made a promise

to take good care of Puppy.

"I think Puppy needs
a real name," said Stella.

"Spot?" asked Mama.

"Puppy has no spots,"
said Stella.

"Fuzzy?" asked Papa.

"Puppy is not fuzzy,"
said Stanley.

"How about Spunky?" said Stella.

"Perfect!" they all agreed.

The Sloths decided to take
Spunky on his first walk
around the block.

They got back home
as the sun came up.
"Home at last," said Stanley.
"With our whole family,"
said all the Sloths.
"Woof!" said Spunky.